Amina of Zaria

The Warrior Queen

Dara Beevas

illustrated by Monique Steele

WISE INK

Dedicated to the Warrior Queens in my life:
My mother, Karen; mother-in-law, Audrey; sisters, Markeda, Kiara, and Sylvia;
and to my favorite li'l warrior queens, Genesis, Sophie, and Marley
—D.B.

To my parents, my siblings, and my niece Azzuneish, and to all those who dare to dream
—M.S.

Hardcover ISBN-13: 978-1-63489-435-7
Paperback ISBN-13: 978-1-63489-436-4
Library of Congress Catalog Number: 2021904110

Printed in the United States of America
First Printing: 2021

25 24 23 22 21 5 4 3 2 1

Cover and interior design by Kim Morehead

Wise Ink Creative Publishing
807 Broadway St NE
Suite 46
Minneapolis, MN, 55413

This Book Belongs to

Queen

______________________________.

My dear li'l queen,

when I was a little girl, I was often overlooked.

Yet I dreamed of becoming a fierce warrior.

Today, I am Queen Amina of Zaria, a beautiful city in Africa. Zaria is a part of Hausa, with the Niger River on one side and Lake Chad on the other.

But I wasn't always a queen. Once I was small like you.

When I was young, my country was always in terrible danger. Invaders from other countries attacked us. They stole from us and took our land.

While others were afraid, I longed to defend my people. I secretly practiced with spears and daggers when no one was watching. You see, princesses were expected to remain at the palace, away from danger. I had other ideas!

One day, Marka, my grandmother, found me playing with a dagger.

"Amina!" she cried. "You hold that dagger with too much comfort, my child."

"Please don't be angry," I whispered.

"Amina, from the moment you were born, I felt in my bones that you would be a mighty queen."

"But *Kaka,* I am a fighter!"

"You will see. Allah has plans for you," she said stubbornly. "You are a warrior. *And* you are the future queen of Zaria. You are brave enough to be both."

Grandmother smiled and let me be. Kings and queens had ruled Zaria, yes. But warriors? I kept my mouth shut, even though I thought Grandmother was very wrong.

Soon I was the best horseback rider east of the Niger River.

I could shoot a bow better than any archer in our army. Some said my arrows traveled hundreds of miles into the bush.

By the time my brother, Karama, became king, I was already a legend.

As the first son, Karama inherited the throne, even though I was older.

Good for him, I thought. *I have battles to fight.*

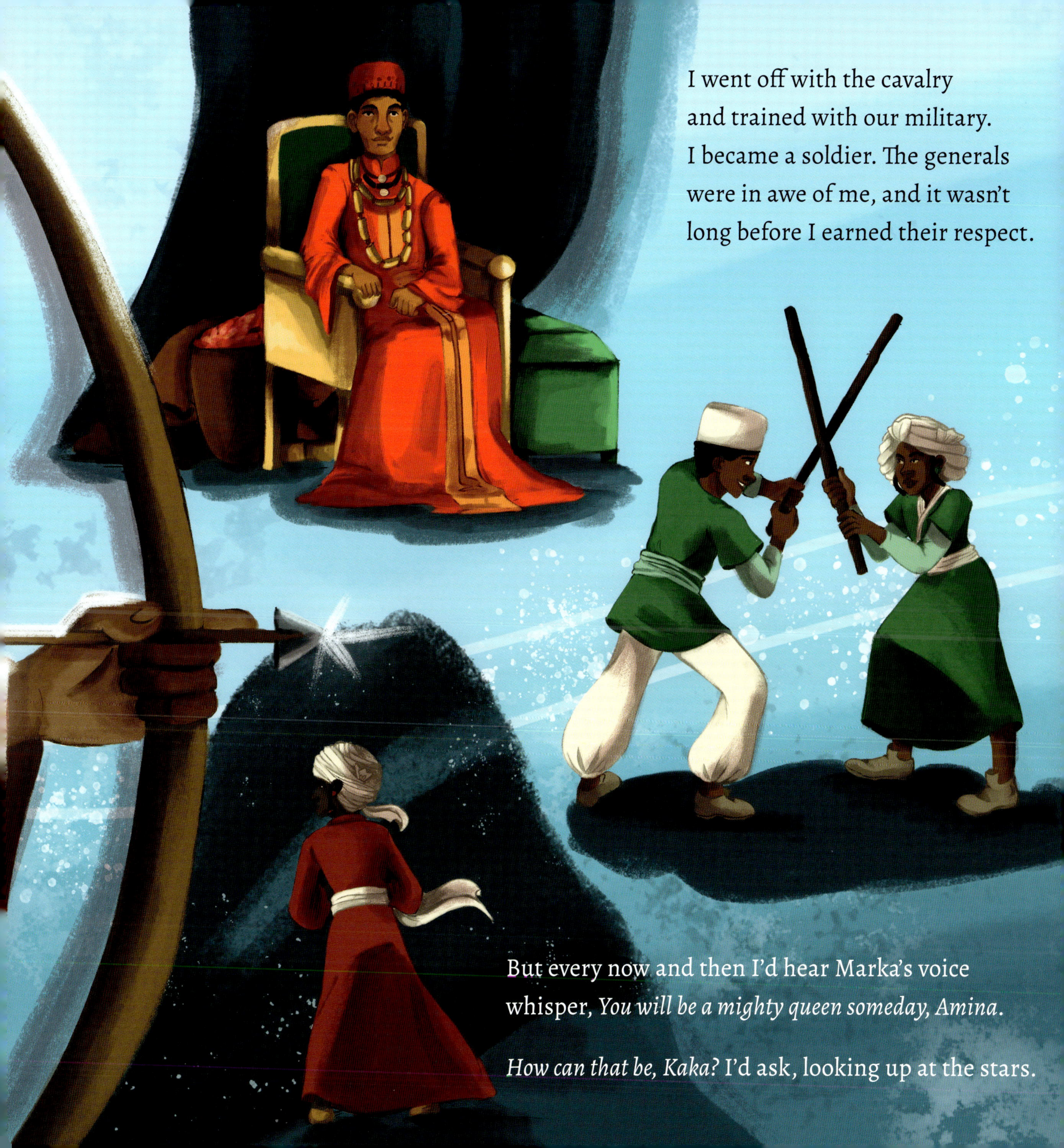

I went off with the cavalry
and trained with our military.
I became a soldier. The generals
were in awe of me, and it wasn't
long before I earned their respect.

But every now and then I'd hear Marka's voice
whisper, *You will be a mighty queen someday, Amina.*

How can that be, Kaka? I'd ask, looking up at the stars.

It wasn't long before I became the leader of Karama's armies.

I mastered every weapon of Zaria's greatest warriors.

Finally, I was the fearless fighter I'd always dreamed of becoming.

Even my horse was fearless. I named her Demon, knowing that our enemies didn't stand a chance against us!

Then Karama became very sick and died. That meant *I* would become queen.

My dear li'l queen, between you and me, I was worried.

I'm a warrior, I thought. *And I'm the best!*

Will Hausa accept a queen who rides horses and fights battles? I'm nothing like Karama or any other king or queen. Warriors belong on the battlefield, not sitting at the palace.

But again, I heard Marka say, *You are brave enough to be both.*

I took my brother's place. As I rode with our armies out to battle, my people cheered, "Amina! Amina! Our mighty warrior queen!"

Marka would have been proud! Mamas held up their daughters to greet me. Papas showed their sons how to hold their spears like Queen Amina.

As our armies became the strongest in the land, I learned that queens come in all shapes and sizes.

Brick by brick, my queendom built tall walls to show people from all over the world how magnificent Zaria is. My people call them *ganuwar Amina*, or “Amina’s walls.”

Because my cities are safe,
people come from all around the Sahara
to buy and sell salt, gold, cloth, and metals.

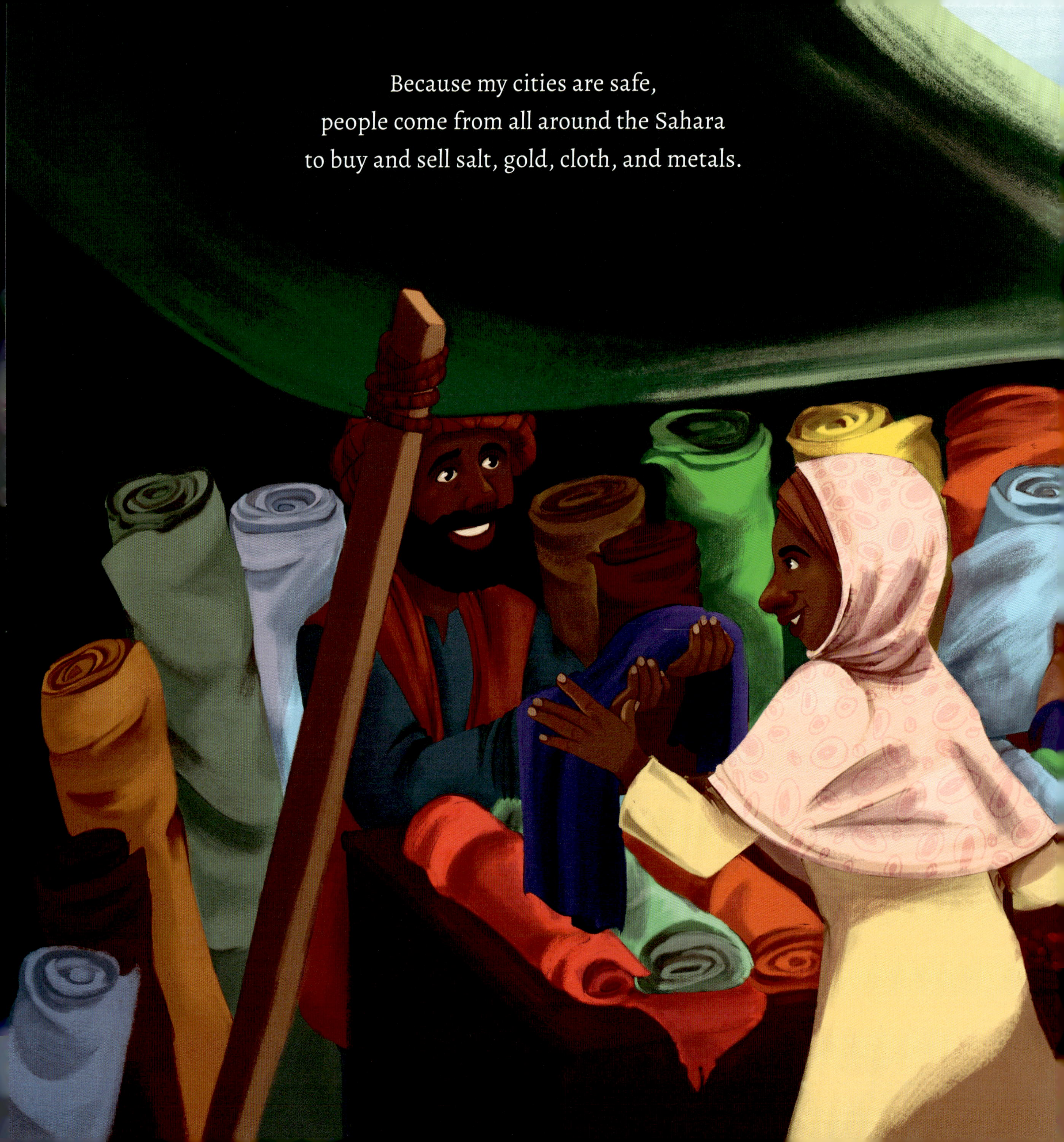

Zaria is one of the wealthiest cities in the land now. Once, I was even given ten thousand kola nuts, a sacred food. Never before had any ruler received such a gift!

Through the years many doubted me. Sometimes, I even doubted myself.

Neighboring cities did not expect me to become so powerful. But my grandmother was right. Queens like you and me are born to do incredible things.

Fighting for what I believe in isn't always easy, li'l queen, but like my mother and other queens before me, I must protect my people.

I rule one of the largest empires in Northern Africa.

We have the fastest horses.

Our armor is strong. My people were among the first in the world to bend metal into helmets.

And you know what? At times I lead more than twenty thousand warriors at once!

My dear li'l queen, I will tell you something my grandmother told me. In our language, Hausa, she said, *"Dole ne ku rayu cikin gaskiyar ku."* That means, "You must live within your sacred truth." Marka would be proud that I am living mine.

I'm a great warrior who is a mighty queen, and I'm a mighty queen who is a great warrior. I am both.

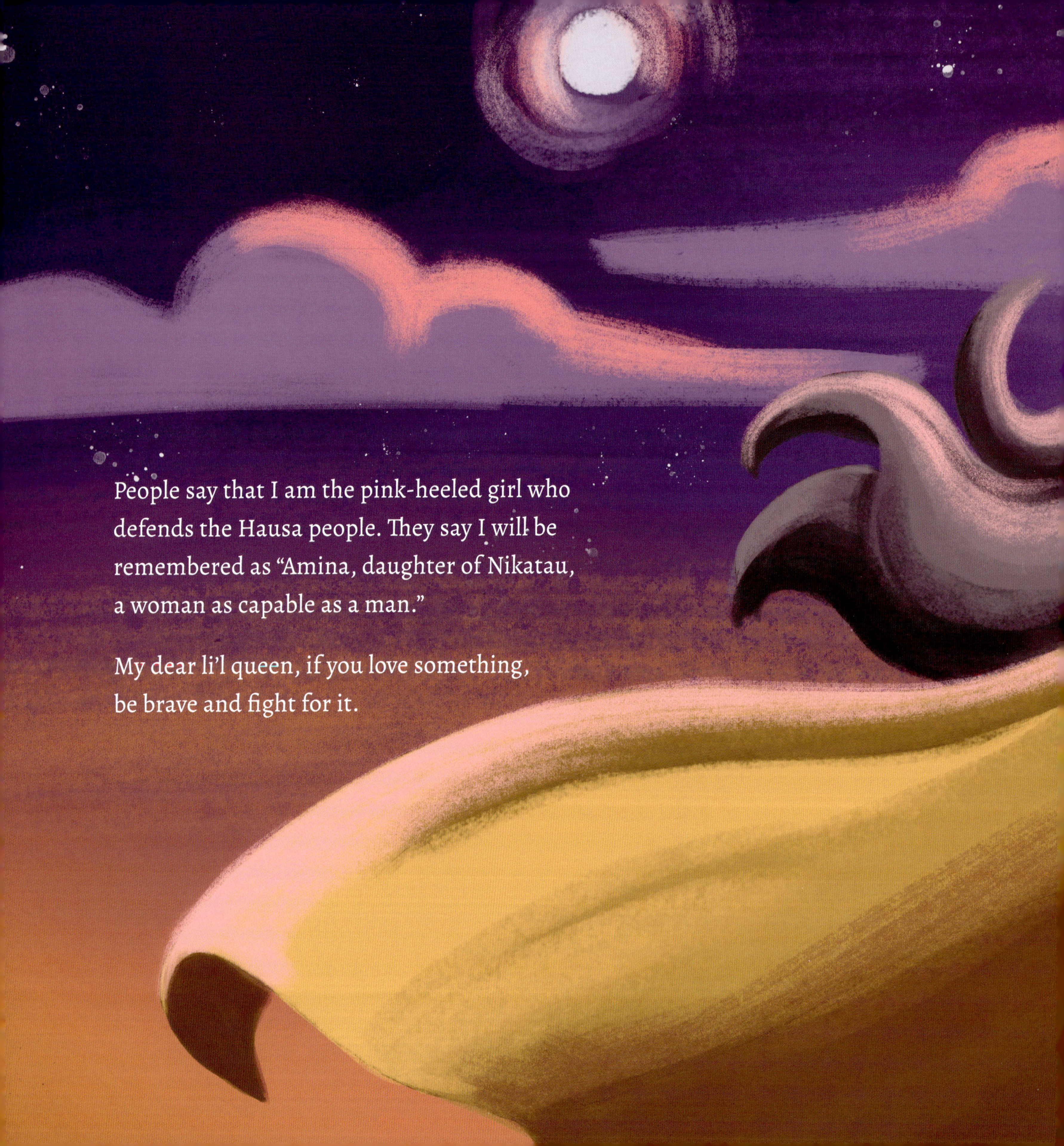

People say that I am the pink-heeled girl who defends the Hausa people. They say I will be remembered as "Amina, daughter of Nikatau, a woman as capable as a man."

My dear li'l queen, if you love something, be brave and fight for it.

I am Queen

____

(write your name)

I was born on ________________ .

I dream of becoming

______________________________ .

I am ____________ , ____________ ,

and ________________________ .

Her Majesty, the Queen

Find your favorite picture of yourself and place it on the mirror. If you're feeling extra creative, draw your self-portrait!

About Queen Amina of Zaria

Queen Amina lived from about 1533–1610. At the time of her reign, Zaria was actually called Zazzau, which was one of seven cities in Hausa. Hausa was constantly under attack because it was right in the middle of three important trade routes to the north, south, and west of where Amina lived.

When Amina became queen, she was no ordinary woman! She was already a known and powerful soldier who had helped to make Zazzau very prosperous. During her brother's ten-year reign, Amina sharpened her battle skills training with the military. Legends say that she mastered every weapon in the armory, including bow and arrows, spears, and swords. Queen Amina ruled for thirty-four years and fought most battles on horseback alongside her army. By the end of her life, she had stretched the boundaries of Hausa further than any other king or queen.

5 Li'l Queen Facts about Queen Amina:

1. There's a statue of Queen Amina in Lagos, Nigeria, with her infamous spear in hand, and with her horse who was actually named Demon.

2. Queen Amina became one of the wealthiest queens of her time. She did this by expanding her empire and making it the trading center of the region.

3. Many of "Amina's Walls" are still standing in Nigeria.

4. Queen Amina refused to get married and never had children. She wanted to focus on winning her battles and keeping her people protected.

5. Queen Amina inspired a television series that aired between 1995–2001 called *Xena: Warrior Princess.*

About the Author

Dara Beevas is an award-winning author, publisher, and speaker with a passion for storytelling. Born in the Washington, DC, area, she earned her master's degree in publishing from George Washington University. Through her books, articles, and presentations, she explores the importance of #diversereads, the power of storytelling, mission-oriented publishing, and startup tips. As a mentor of more than four hundred authors and publisher of more than three hundred books, she pushes executives, storytellers, innovators, and change agents to publish mindfully. *Amina of Zaria: The Warrior Queen* is the first in the Li'l Queens series to raise more than twenty thousand dollars on Kickstarter. Dara lives in Minneapolis with her husband, Tomme, and their two children, Genesis and Derek.

To follow the series, download free Li'l Queens tools, and purchase books, visit www.darabeevas.com.

About the Illustrator

Monique Steele is a Jamaican-born illustrator currently residing in NYC. Thematically, her art focuses mostly on exploring historical costuming, fan culture, and diabolical women in power. When she's not drawing famous queens in history, you can find her deeply mired in the comings and goings of pop culture, trying to refine her spicy foods palette and lamenting no longer living the "island girl" lifestyle.

Li'l Queens Hall of Fame

Aaliyah Outley
Abigail Marsh
Ally Sage
Amina Ward
Anna Cheng
Annette Brown
Audrey Beevas
Azzuneish Steele
Barbara Hembry
Chantelle Bevas
De'Mario Steele
Dahlia Oliver
Dr. Joi Lewis
Ebony Bristol
Emery Walker
Emily Balogh
Esmin Adams
Genesis Irene Beevas
Hava Nornang Kampe
Irene Lewis
Jada Gordon
Jade Christie
Janelle Jones
Jeanelle Leon
Jennifer Brown Bennett
Kali Ward
Karen Brown
Kate Davenport
Katrina Brown
Kiara Hembry
Kristen Brown
Lena Benson
Lyric Mychael Higgins
Maisha Diercks
Makeda-Malia Clark
Markeda Brown
Marley Ennette Brown
Natakia Bevas
Nina-Symone Kezia Robinson
Olivia Farrell
Oluwakemi Mary-Jennifer Oyedele
Patricia Pete
Paul Steele
Primrose Lynch
Queenie Bevas
Rosa Magnone
Rose Nzinga Harris
Rylee Ogunlade
Sasha Cassadine
Shanaya Eady
Shirice Harris
Steven Steele
Stevi Chalmers
Sylvia Beevas
Tamara Marsh
Trinity Sophie Laydonna Smith
Vicky Gonzalez
Violet-Hazel Lynch
Zharia Bell Myles
Zhuri-Bella Bristol
Zoe Steinman

A Special Message from our Legacy Backers:

In loving memory of Milt Adams
—Susan Adams Loyd

In honor of my favorite li'l queens: Aleice, Lela, Seanna, and Aubrie
—Carnell Cherry